Dear Parent:

Your child's love of reading starts here!

Every child learns to read in a different way and at his or her own speed. Some go back and forth between reading levels and read favorite books again and again. Others read through each level in order. You can help your young reader improve and become more confident by encouraging his or her own interests and abilities. From books your child reads with you to the first books he or she reads alone, there are I Can Read Books for every stage of reading:

SHARED READING
Basic language, word repetition, and whimsical illustrations, ideal for sharing with your emergent reader

BEGINNING READING
Short sentences, familiar words, and simple concepts for children eager to read on their own

READING WITH HELP
Engaging stories, longer sentences, and language play for developing readers

READING ALONE
Complex plots, challenging vocabulary, and high-interest topics for the independent reader

I Can Read Books have introduced children to the joy of reading since 1957. Featuring award-winning authors and illustrators and a fabulous cast of beloved characters, I Can Read Books set the standard for beginning readers.

A lifetime of discovery begins with the magical words "I Can Read!"

Visit www.icanread.com for information
on enriching your child's reading experience.

Pinkalicious®
and the Pinkettes

To Amara and Cordelia
—V.K.

The author gratefully acknowledges
the artistic and editorial contributions of
Daniel Griffo and Jacqueline Resnick.

Pinkalicious and the Pinkettes
Copyright © 2020 by VBK, Co.

Based on the HarperCollins book *Pinkalicious* written by
Victoria Kann and Elizabeth Kann, illustrated by Victoria Kann

ISBN 978-0-06-284051-6 (trade bdg.)—ISBN 978-0-06-284050-9 (pbk.)

20 21 22 23 24 LSCC 10 9 8 7 6 5 4 3 2 1
❖
First Edition

I Can Read!

1 BEGINNING READING

Pinkalicious®
and the Pinkettes

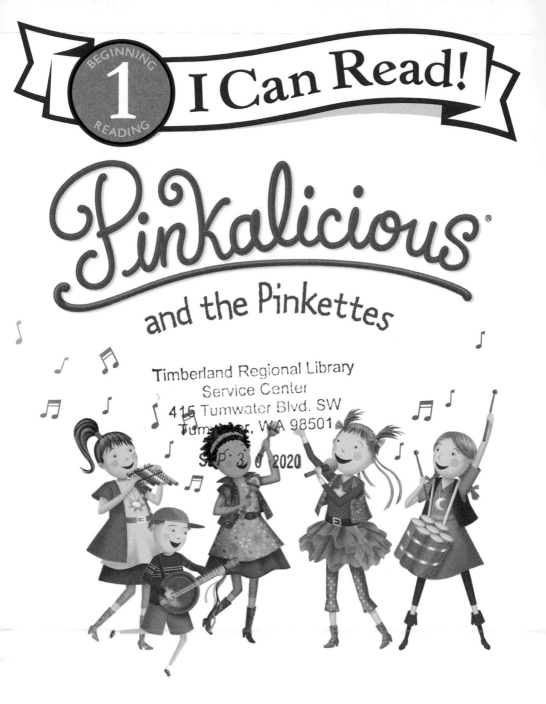

by Victoria Kann

HARPER
An Imprint of HarperCollinsPublishers

My friends and I were in the park
when I heard my favorite song.
"Kendra's band is rocktastic!"
I said.

"Let's dance to the music,"

Molly said.

We twirled and spun.

"I wish we had a band,"

Alison said.

"Me, too," I said.

"Let's start our own band!"

When the song was over

I said to Kendra,

"We're starting a band, too!"

"What kind of instruments

do you have?" asked Kendra.

"Umm," Molly said.

"We don't have any," Alison said.

Kendra looked confused.

"How can you play music

without any instruments?" she asked.

"Kendra's right," Rose said sadly.
"How can we have a band
without instruments?"
I sat down to think.
The park was noisy.

A boy bounced a ball with a *thump*!

A girl rang her bicycle bell.

The bell made a *rinnnggg* sound.

I closed my eyes and listened.

Thump! Ring! Thump! Ring!

13

"Do you hear that?"

I asked my friends.

"When those noises come together,

it sounds like music!"

"It even has a beat," Molly said.

"I know how we can have a band,"
I said.

"We can make our instruments!"

We went to my house

to get materials.

"What can we use to make

sounds?"

Alison asked.

"Tons of things

make great sounds," I said.

"Like these spoons," Rose said.

She drummed on the table.

"That sounds like music!" I said.

Rose scraped a fork on a bottle.

"EEK, that doesn't sound good!"

Molly said.

Alison banged on a pot.

"Too loud!" I said.

18

"I guess we need to find

the right sound." I giggled.

Molly shook a homemade rattle.

"Now that's pinkapretty!" I said.

We kept working until

we each had our own sound.

19

We went to the park
to try out our new instruments.
"Come hear us play!"
I said to Kendra.

"Play what?" Kendra asked.

"Are those supposed

to be instruments?"

I looked at Kendra's fancy guitar

and then at my homemade banjo.

Suddenly our new instruments

didn't seem so great.

"I don't think our instruments
are good enough.
We can't be a band," I said sadly.
I dragged myself home.

"Did you make that?" Peter asked

when he saw my banjo.

"Can I try it?"

He danced as he strummed.

"That looks fun," Rose said.

Rose, Molly, and Alison joined Peter.
Mommy and Daddy came to listen.
"Sing a song, Pinkalicious!"
Daddy said.

"One, two, three, four,

Pinkville rocks forevermore!"

I sang.

"You sound like a real band!

Bravo!" Mommy said.

"Introducing the Pinkettes," I said.

"Band hug!" Molly said.

"We sound like rock stars," I said.

"Now we need to look

like rock stars!"

"Let's meet in the park,"

Rose said.

"Dressed like the Pinkettes!"

"I'm coming, too," Peter said.

Our band was ready.

"Time to rock and roll," I said.

We got the beat and added a melody.

We were making music!

It was so much fun,

I barely noticed a crowd had formed.

"Look at Kendra!"

Rose said suddenly.

"Wow," I said.

"She's dancing to our music!"

THE PINKETTES

"Go, Pinkettes!" Kendra cheered.

"I guess you don't need fancy

instruments to make music!"

"Do you know what's better

than one band?" I asked Kendra.

"TWO bands together!"

Kendra's band joined ours.

Their speakers made our music

so loud that it could be heard

all over Pinkville.

Everyone sang together.

"One, two, three, four,

Pinkville rocks forevermore!"